SHERLEY ANNE WILLIAMS

GIRLS TOGETHER

Paintings by
SYNTHIA
SAINT JAMES

HARCOURT BRACE & COMPANY
San Diego   New York   London

Library of Congress Cataloging-in-Publication Data
Williams, Sherley Anne, 1944—
Girls together/written by Sherley Anne Williams; illustrated by Synthia Saint James.—1st ed.
p.   cm.
Summary: Five young girls from a housing project spend a day playing together.
ISBN 0-15-230982-9
[1. Friendship—Fiction. 2. Inner cities—Fiction. 3. City and town life—Fiction.]
I. Saint James, Synthia, ill. II. Title.
PZ7.W668174Gi   1999
[E]—dc20   95-31788

First edition
A C E F D B

Printed in Singapore

The illustrations in this book were done in acrylic paints on canvas.
The display type was set in Tool Cities.
The text type was set in Bernhard Gothic.
Color separations by Tien Wah Press, Singapore
Printed and bound by Tien Wah Press, Singapore
This book was printed on totally chlorine-free Nymolla Matte Art paper.
Production supervision by Stanley Redfern and Ginger Boyer
Designed by Linda Lockowitz

One summer morning we get up real early, before anyone else in our house. We wash and dress real quiet. Mamma hear, she sure to find us something to do.

Sun just barely looking and everything
quiet except for the birds. Air feel like if you
fell into a trailer full of cotton; it's just that
soft on your skin.

Hattie Jean, ViLee, and Lois live down
the Project from Ruise and me. We almost
like stairsteps.

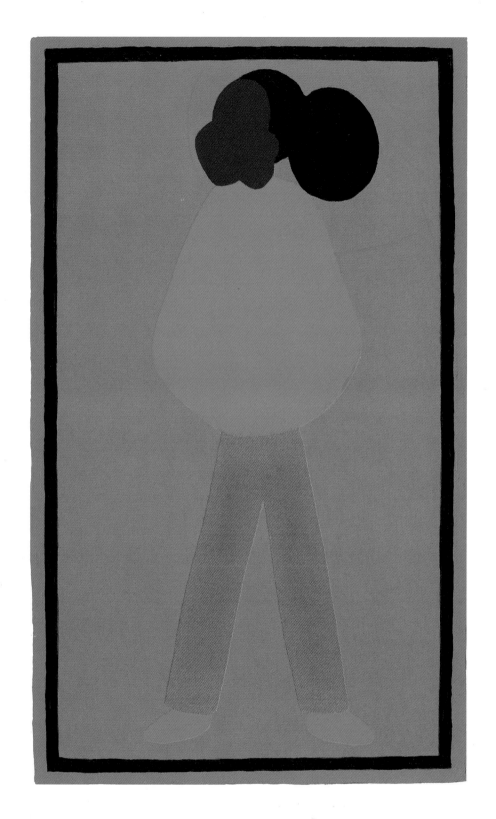

Ruise, the oldest, skinny as a snake, have a grin make you grin with her, her teeth so white and straight.

Lois is the tallest, so dark she look black, her face
pretty as any doll's. She got to stay inside till her
mother or father come home from work. She can't have
no friends in her house till then.

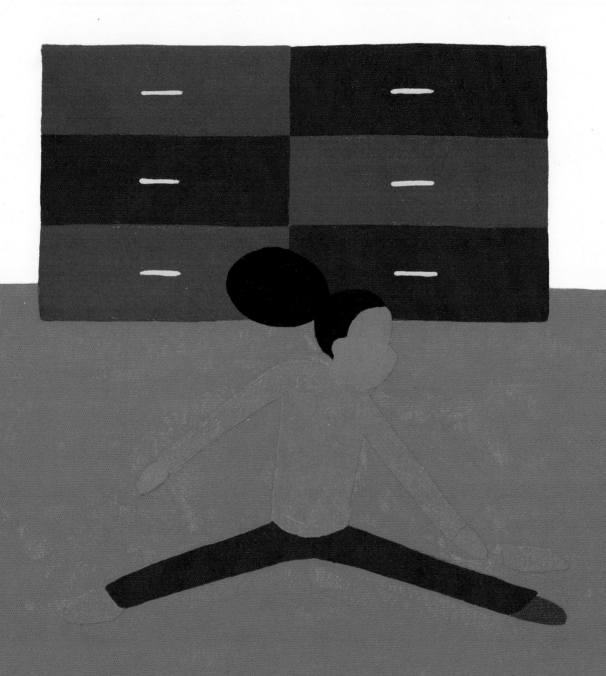

Hattie Jean one year older than me. She like a little beanpole, knobby knees and arms, and so limber she can do just about any dance.

We draw paper dolls and play dress-up at Hattie Jean's house. She have a room all to herself.

ViLee the same age as me, though she still got a lot of baby fat. She wear her hair in three long plaits. My hair is short, my cheeks dimple when I smile.

ViLee say, Let's go; Mamma catch me in the Project,
I have to take Buster with us. Buster her baby brother,
tell everything he know. Let's ride bikes, she say.

Sometimes we take turns hiking each other on Hattie Jean's and ViLee's bikes. Once we went almost all the way to Roding Park before our legs give out and we had to turn back.

Hattie Jean's bike is on a flat and Ruise and me don't have one.

We could collect bottles for the recycler. I want
to find enough for the dollar movie on Saturday. I like
the pictures with singing in them. Sometimes we
make pretend and act out stories, try new dance
steps, put our own words to the songs.

We ought to stay where we can hear Mamma when she call us. Ruise take my hand but I don't want to go home.

Maybe some grown-up have an errand for us to run.

Sometimes a grown person do pay a little something for our help or send to the store and let us keep the change. But ViLee just don't want to stay around where Buster is.

Let's go climb trees, Hattie Jean say; that's not too far to walk.

We leave out the Project, all us girls together.
Hey, hey, we say, and link arms when we walk.

It's no houses round the Project; just a vacant lot, a truck company, some empty buildings, the Legion, where

grown people dance on Friday and Saturday nights. You

These houses not all that big; just plain people live here. Hattie Jean say it wasn't so early we'd see them outside. It all look like a picture to me—gingerbread houses, grass green as crayon and so thick it about cover

up your feet when you step on it, all these trees a fairy-
tale forest.

Seem like it could be some story behind even a plain
brown door.

Ruise know the names of trees. Sycamore have little
fuzzy balls that itch like crazy they get on your arm or
leg. Pines look like great big Christmas trees, but they
mostly in people's yards, so we don't climb them much.

The flower tree she call magnolia, blossoms big and
white on shiny dark-green leaves. It's the most fun to
climb; the branches not way over my head and the
flowers smell about as good as perfume.

The flowers not really white, more like pale butter or vanilla ice cream. The petals turn brown if you put your fingers on them too much.
The petals feel like velvet against my face.

You supposed to put it in your hair, Hattie Jean say.
She pin a flower upside her head and pose.
Movie star, movie star, we tell her. Laughing and

posing now, Ruise thread a flower stem through ViLee's
braids; I stick mines behind my ear.
　　Let's take this one to Lois, ViLee say.

Lois look real pretty in a white flower hair barrette.